Isaac Asklöf

An Essay on the Romance of William and the Werwolf

A specimen of the Midland dialect in the middle of the 14th century

Isaac Asklöf

An Essay on the Romance of William and the Werwolf
A specimen of the Midland dialect in the middle of the 14th century

ISBN/EAN: 9783337736637

Printed in Europe, USA, Canada, Australia, Japan

Cover: Foto ©Andreas Hilbeck / pixelio.de

More available books at **www.hansebooks.com**

AN ESSAY

ON

THE ROMANCE OF WILLIAM AND THE WERWOLF.

A SPECIMEN OF THE MIDLAND DIALECT IN THE MIDDLE
OF THE 14:TH CENTURY.

I.

ACADEMICAL DISSERTATION
FOR OBTAINING OF THE PHILOSOPHICAL DEGREE

BY

ISAAC ASKLÖF, PHIL. CAND.
OSTROG.

WITH PERMISSION OF THE PHILOSOPHICAL FACULTY PUBLICLY DISCUSSED
AT THE LARGER GUSTAVIAN AUDITORY IN UPSALA
MAY 4, 1872 AT 4 O'CLOCK P. M.

STOCKHOLM
PRINTED BY G. W. BLOMQVIST
1872.

INTRODUCTION.

The Romance of William and the Werwolf, the language of which we are about to treat, is supposed to have been written about the year 1360. Its dialect is the Midland-English dialect (Shropshire) and belongs to the period of the English language which is called Middle-English. — Concerning the author of this romance, we know nothing, except that he lived during the reign of king Edward II, at the command of whose nephew Humphrey de Bohun, Earl of Hereford, he translated his work from the French. Let us for a while fix our attention on this circumstance that the romance in question was translated from the French. If we regard the word *romance*, we shall at once understand, that this species of literature had not its origin in England, but must on the contrary have been introduced from the Romance countries, that is to say from France, Italy or Spain [1]), where the Romance languages especially are spoken. The English word *romance*, It. *romanzo*, Sp. *romance*, Pr., O. Fr. *romans*, M. Lat. *romancium* are derived from the Lat. adverb *romanice*, as it is also used in O. Fr. *parler romans*, loqui romanice [2]).

We will now endeavour to give a literary view of the English poetry, and especially of the romances, during the Middle age. During the first period of the English language, comprehending the greater part of the thirteenth and about half of the fourteenth century, the English poets may be divided into two classes, the first composing me-

---

[1] We have not mentioned Portugal, the Danube provinces and Graubündten, their literature being during the Middle age of no importance.
[2] See Diez, Wörterbuch der Romanischen Sprachen.

trical lives of the saints or rhyming chronicles, the second
satirical pieces and love-songs. Tales of chivalry were to
a certain degree a subject, common to them both. As to
the origin of the romantic fiction, there are two different
opinions, the one pretends that the romantic fiction is originally Gothic, or Celtic, the other that it is originally
Oriental. Of the first opinion is Bishop Percy, who in
his »Reliquies of ancient English poetry»[3] speaks in the
following manner: »The minstrels seem to have been the
genuine successors of the ancient bards, who, under different names, were admired and revered, from the earliest
ages, among the people of the Gaul, Britain, Ireland and
the North and indeed by almost all the first inhabitants of
Europe, whether of Celtic or Gothic race, but by none
more than by our own Danish tribes. Among these they
were distinguished by the names of *Scalds*, a word which
denotes »smoothers and polishers of language» The origin
of their art was attributed to Odin or Wodan, the father
of their gods, and the professors of it were held in the
highest estimation.» Thus Bishop Percy evidently thinks
the romantic fiction to be of Gothic (or Celtic) origin, as
the minstrels were from the North. In his essay on the
ancient metrical, romances Percy says among other argu-
ments against the opinion, that the romantic fiction is from
the Orient, that »it seems utterly incredible, that one rude
people should adopt a peculiar taste and manner of writing or thinking from the other, without borrowing at
the same time any of their particular stories and fables,
without appearing to know any thing of their laws, heroes
history and religion». Mr. Warton on the contrary, sought
to prove, that the romantic fiction had ist origin in the
Orient and that the Arabs, during their plundering expe-
ditions through Europe, had brought to the European people the material to their songs. Doubtless, much of Oriental origin can be traced in the poetry of this period, but
as Mr. Dunlop (in his History of fiction) has made very
evident, the romances have traces of both Oriental and
Gothic origin. We are also of the opinion that, especi-

---

[3] Part I, p. XXII.

ally during the crusades, when several Arabian tales, fables and songs found their way to Europe, they had an influence on the fancy of the minstrels and troubadours, which gave another colour to their songs. Thus it is that we can trace both Gothic and Oriental elements in the romances of the Middle age.

Having thus spoken of the origin of the romantic fiction, we will return to the English romances. It was especially in France and Spain that the romance poetry flourished. Consequently the English romances were, nearly all, mere translations from French, and so is, as has been stated above, the case with *the Romance of William and the Werwolf*. It was from Normandy, that the earliest compositions in the English language came, being translations from the Norman poets. But before the English language did exist, the literary products were written in French (and Latin) and even long afterwards. The French language was at that time, as it is still, familiar to all persons of the higher classes throughout the continental Europe and Great Britain and was therefore a convenient medium of communication between them. Thus many foreign authors wrote their works in French, as for example Brunetto Latini, the teacher of Dante, writing his most important work in French, in stead of Italian, thus apologizes his using the French language: »Et se aucune demandoit por coi cest liures est escrit en romãs selonc le pacoys de france, puis que nos comēsames ytalliens, ie diroie que ce est por diuerses raisons; l'une que nos somes en france et l'autre por ce q̃ la parleur est plus delitable et plus comune a tous lengages.« In English it may be thus translated: And if any one should ask, why this book is written in Romance, according to the patois of France, I being born Italian, I shall say that it is for several reasons; one is that I am now in France and the other that this language is the most delightful and partakes most of the common nature of all languages.

We may not therefore wonder, that many English writers wrote their works in French and sometimes even in Provençal, only from literary considerations. There are even poems, written partly in English and partly in French.

A poem from 1311 for example, commences with a stanza
in both languages, which we will represent here, as it is
given by Mr.' Marsh (Origin and History of the Engl.
Language p. 244).

> L'en puet fere et defere
> Ceo fait-il trop souvent
> It nis nouther wel ne faire;
> Therfore Engelond is shent
> Nostre prince de Engleterre,
> Par le consail de sa gent,
> At Westminster after the feire
> Made a gret parlemeut.
> La chartre fet de cyre,
> Jeo l'enteink et bien le crey
> It was holde to neih the fire,
> And is melten al awey.
> Ore ne say mès que dire
> Tout i va a Tripolay
> Hundred, chapitle, cour and shire,
> Al hit goth a devel way.
> Des plusages de la tere
> Ore escotez un sarmoun,
> Of iij wise-men that ther were,
> Whi Engelond is brouht adoun.

But though, as we have sought to prove most products
of the English literature, during its earliest period, were
mere translations from the French, we should be wrong,
were we to maintain the opinion, that the early English
literature was only an imitation from French or Norman
authors. It was not even in the kingdom of France that
French poetry commenced to be cultivated. On the contrary, it was from England and Normandy, according to
M. de la Rue, that the French received the first literarary
products of any value in their language. The Normans
were of a Northern race, and could not during that time
be considered as French, though they spoke the French
language. It was from the Norman poets that the earliest
English writers translated their works. But the English

monarchs were themselves »the most liberal and perhaps the earliest patrons of English poetry»[4]. Thus it is that Mr. Marsh calls the earliest English poetry an imitation from Norman or French; he will not count the numerous ballads and national songs as a literature, and consequently says: »there was and could be no national literature, until the latter half of the fourteenth century». Notwithstanding the high merits of Mr. Marsh's researches on the early English language and literature, we cannot on this point fully agree with him, for the early English ballads, which had sprung out from a Teutonic people, have a dramatic element and often a tragical sublimity, which is not to be found in the French poetry. England had in its ballads and songs rich sources to a national literature, which some centuries afterwards brought forth the great poet, who »surpassed all efforts of ancient and modern genius». Certainly these ballads and songs were not written in the same dialect, for there were several different dialects in England, and none of them had gained supremacy on the other, for no great author had yet arisen; and it was not till the time of Edward III, that the English language became fixed and deserved to be called a written speech. As a distinction between the early English literature and other imaginative literatures, we may remark, that the English literature took a more practical aim, and concerned more the social being of man and the development of his character. — The romances, as we have said, came chiefly from France, where they were intimately connected with chivalry, which through the Normans was at first introduced into England. Thus it was the knights and their ladies that enjoyed these romances, but gradually they came into the mouths of the people, where they survived much longer than amongst the families of the barons and knights.

Before treating the language in the romance of William and the Werwolf, we regard it as necessary to give a short account of the English language during the earlier time down to the period, when this romance was written.

---

[4] Ellis, Specimens of the early English poets.

vated, than that of the Anglo-Saxons, at least there are many poetical products, written in that dialect, which have come down to us.

During the first century after the conquest there existed in England chiefly three languages. The language of the king and nobles was Norman-French, that of the church Latin and that of the people Anglo-Saxon, not to mention the languages of the Celtic inhabitants of England. As there existed a mutual hatred between the oppressors and the oppressed race, it was impossible for the one language to arise to supremacy over the other, for as the Normans despised the Saxons, so did the Anglo-Saxons dispise the Normans in their turn, and considered therefore the language as a foreign one, and both languages very carefully avoided words from foreign origin.

Gradually, however, the Anglo-Saxon language lost its purity, and we are at a new development in this language, which may be called Semi-Saxon, and extended from 1150 to 1250, according to Mr. Marsh. As we have said before, the Anglo-Saxon language was after the conquest only spoken by the common people, but Norman-French was the language of the higher classes and consequently became the language, used by government and at law.

The language called Semi-Saxon grew up, when Anglo-Saxon had dropped some inflections and had begun to use newly developed auxiliaries. But even throughout this period the two languages existed side by side, though the fusion of the dialects had begun, and, in truth, none of them could yet be considered as the standard of the national tongue.

The most important work, written in Semi-Saxon, is Layamon's translation of Brut d'Angleterre. This translation was made in the year 1185. The language of this book is very different from the old Anglo-Saxon. As an instance we may remark, that Layamon, in his construction of the verb, very regularly employs *shall* and *will* as technical auxiliaries. We remark also, that the Scandinavian form *aren* plural. pres. of the verb *beon* (to be) occurs for the first time in »the Ormulum», written during this period.

Thus the Saxon language began dropping the old Anglo-Saxon inflectious and employing more liberally particles and determinatives. We do not pretend to say that the language won anything in beauty by the said change. On the contrary, Comden says: »Great, verily, was the glory of our tongue, before the Norman conquest, in this, that the old English could express, most aptly, all the conceptions of mind in their own tongue, without borrowing from any.»

Though the Norman-French long rivalled with the Saxon, yet is was impossible to change absolutely the vernacular tongue. But out of the intermarriages between Normans and Saxons a new Teutonic people grew up, which began to be proud of their English name and out of the fusion of the two languages a new arose.

The next period in the history of the English language is called Old-English between 1250 and 1350. It was during that period that Anglo-Saxon and French was forming the English language; and in this fusion the Saxon element prevailed and formed the grammatical structure of the English language. This period is then the first, during which an English language can be said to exist, for during the last foregoing Semi-Saxon period, the language was a degenerated Anglo-Saxon. But it is, naturally, quite impossible to fix a distinct period, when the Saxon language did cease and the English begun, especially as there were no authoritative standards in the literature of these times, and, moreover, there are very few printed literary monuments from the thirteenth century, though that century is one of the most important in the history of the English language.

The new language was not spoken in the same manner over all England, but it grew up in different dialects, owing to local circumstances. It was chiefly three dialects, that maintained their place in the literature, namely, the Northern, the Midland and the Southern dialects. As we have stated above, there existed yet no authoritative literary standard, and, consequently, no dialect could become the general language of England during the thirteenth century. — One of the most important writers during the Old-English period was Robert of Gloucester, who wrote his work in a Southern dialect.

The most remarkable novelties in the language during this period are the present plural termination in *en* instead af *th* and the use of the plural pronoun, in adressing a single person. As to this use, we may remark, that both the singular and the plural pronoun were employed indiscriminately even for some centuries after this period.

The next era in the English language extended according to Mr. Marsh, from 1350 to the third quarter of the sixteenth century and is called Middle-English. We have remarked, that there are very few literary remains of importance from the preceding period, but we are nevertheless of the opinion, that the beginning of the English literature falls into the thirteenth century. — In the Middle-English period there existed, without doubt, a vernacular literature, as well as a native language. The people had now learnt to be proud of their English name, and the new idiom was now distinctly different from other languages. In its grammar it is yet Teutonic, and it is strange to find, that during this period, though the authors, being most of them, as we have mentioned above, translators from French or Latin, introduced many foreign, especially French and Latin, words into the English tongue, they employed nevertheless in the syntax many Anglo-Saxon forms, which had nearly grown obsolete, and the grammatical structure took no influence from foreign languages.

As to the introduction of Latin words, we may remark, that though some of them have been directly borrowed from Latin, yet the greatest part of them have been introduced through the medium of French and Italian. The scientific words are chiefly borrowed from Greek.

It was the wars of Edward III that chiefly awakened the national spirit and brought forth many products of the vernacular literature.

In Middle-English most of the romances were written. As these, as we have remarked, were often translations from French, Romance poetry gained a great influence upon the

English writers, who began employing Romance systems of verse and, with few exceptions to omit the old Saxon rhymes. Many French words were, of course, introduced through these writers.

As the principal authors of this period wrote their works in the Southern dialect, it was natural, that this dialect should become the idiom of the literature. As a South-English peculiarity, we remark the termination *-th* in third person present indicative singular and frequently in all persons of the plural of the verbs. This termination is used by Chaucer and many other contemporaneous secular writers.

As we have stated above, the Romance of *William and the Werwolf* was written during the last mentioned period of the English language.

We do not intend to speak of the literary value of the Romance of William and the Werwolf. But now proceeding to the chief purpose of this dissertation, being to make some researches on the above-mentioned romance, we will, at first, give some general remarks on its dialect. This romance is written, as we have mentioned before, in the West-Midland dialect of Shropshire, and as this dialect has very much contributed to the development of the present written English, it will be interesting to observe the prominent features of it, as it is employed in this romance.

The romance of William and the Werwolf being written during the Middle-English period, many old forms are, of course, retained, while, on the other hand, many inflections are dropped.

The spelling is, as during the whole transition period, very indefinite, not to say arbitrary, the same words being spelled in a different manner by the same author. Thus, for instance, we find in »William and the Werwolf»: *happe*, v. 30 and *hap* v. 192; *soþe* and *sothe*, ex. »I wol you telle, as swithe the sothe», v. 104, and »soþe for to telle» v. 32, and a great mass of others.

Originally we intended to compare somewhat completely the vowels and the consonants in this romance with those of the New-English and the Ang.-Saxon, but as this would take away too much of our time and surpass the sheets, allotted to this dissertation, we will confine ouselves to a few remarks. Some others will be given in the linguistic treatise of the verbs.

The Angl.-Saxon letter »þ» is often retained, but is sometimes changed to *th*, as we have seen from the above written example *). Instead of the New-Engl. letters *gh* the A. S. letter »ꟗ« is nearly always employed, especially before *t*, and at the end of words. Ex. wiꟗtliche (quickly) v. 63; hiꟗt (promised) v. 56. At the end of words »ꟗ« had formerly the sound of the Gr. χ or Germ. *ch*, and was probably so pronounced during the Middle-English period. In Modern Engl. it is most often replaced by »*gh*«. — Moreover, the letter ꟗ is often employed, where M. E. has »g« or »y«. Ex. ꟗerne, v. 56 (to desire) Mod. Engl. *yearne;* »be ꟗe sure«, v. 72; ꟗe from Angl. S. *ge;* Mod. Engl. *ye;* ꟗif. Mod. Engl. *give;* ꟗa v. 315, Mod. Eng *yea* and ꟗif (if) v. 313. The third person feminine is sometimes spelled ꟗhe (Angl. S. heô), as v. 117: »nede nadde ꟗhe mamore of nigromauncy to lere« (nor had *she* anything more of negromancy to learn). The letter »ꟗ« thus always replaced a guttural sound. **) There is also in this romance always used an old Anglo-Saxon abbreviation instead of *and.* but as it is not to be had, it has been in this essay replaced by the word *and.*

Respecting the employment of the vowels in this romance, we remark the following peculiarities.

The vowel *a* seems to have more often retained its purity in the dialect of this romance, than in the Southern dialect, perhaps owing to some influence from the North. It is used instead of M. E. *e: wanne,* v. 9, *whan,* v. 26.; Mod. Engl. *when;* þan, v. 15, Mod. Engl. *then;* it is also sometimes employed instead of Mod. E. *ea: radely,* v. 39, Mod. Eng. *readily;* instead of Modern Eng. *o: fellawes* v. 183, M. Engl. *fellows;* quaþ v. 240, Mod. E. *quoth* Swed *qvad; wan* v. 179 Mod. E. won; a. s. o.

But sometimes *a* has changed to *e: mey;* v. 22, Mod. E. *may; hert* v. 8, Engl. *heart; pertelyche* v. 51, but also *parteliche* v. 94.

---

*) The use of this letter was continued as late as the 16th century. See Rask; Anglo-Saxon Grammar, p. 4.

**) The letter "ꟗ", representing the softer sound of "g", from its similitude in form to "z" has, in the printed copies of Old Engl. and Middle Engl., and especially of Scotch, ignorantly been represented with that character and so pronounced. See Percy: "Reliquies of ancient English Poetry", where it is printed as *z.*

The original vowel is also often retained, so that no rules hereupon can be given, as the use fluctuates.

We have already remarked the interchange of the vowel *e* with *a*. Where New Engl. has short *e*, stands often *i*, especially in the prefix *be*, for ex.: *bifel* v. 1; *bi-tide* v. 5; *bitok* v. 64; bihold v. 46, *bi* (imperat. of *be*) v. 311; *hire-self* v. 368 (obs. the Anglo-Saxon possessive femin. form *hire*). Nevertheless the use fluctuates; thus the *e* is used in many words, quite as in New Eng.; for example: *behoued* v. 14, and many others; the vowel *i* must in these instances be considered as original, but there are also examples that this *i* has softened to *e* in some words, where Mod. E. has retained the original vowel, for ex.: *leved* v. 80, Mod. E. *lived* a. o.

We have shown, that the vowel *i* is retained in several words in this dialect, where it has softened to *e* in Mod. E.; besides that, we remark, that it occurs very often, that the *i* has changed to *y*, for ex. »*y* am holde» v. 306; »not y» v. 509; »y ne kan hem gelde» v. 310; *seyde* v. 343; *kyn* v. 354 (Eng. *kin); kyndely* v. 12; but we also meet with the vowel *i*, seldom softened to *e*, where Mod. E. has *y*; f. ex, *semliche* v. 47; Mod. E. *seemly; lobli* v. 48, Mod. E. *loathly; mani* v. 101. a) The letter *e* is seldom employed, where Mod. E. has short *i*; compare the above mentioned example *leved.*

The vowel *o* is employed nearly in the same manner as in Mod. E., especially where this vowel is long. Only a few remarks are to be made; *o* is frequently dropped before *u*, and sometimes before *w*, when the syllable is short: f. ex. *cuntre* v. 4; *schuld* v. 133; *sorwe* (sorrow) v. 84; *fulwes* v. 31: *folwe* v. 178; *fond* (found) v. 71; but it is also sometimes retained; as for ex.: *savour* v. 27; *o* sometimes occurs, where Mod. Eng. has *a*; for ex. *wommon* v. 65; farre *londes* v. 153; »y con þe gret *thonke*» v. 286. As to the vowel *u*,

---

a) In the renowned ancient ballad of Chevy-Chase the vowel *y* is still more often employed instead of *i* or even *e;* for ex. *syde* v. 24, Mod. Eng. *side; promys* v. 25; *Chyviat* v. 27; *comynge* v. 41; *Ynglonde* v. 85 a. s. o. See Percy, Reliquies of ancient English Poetry, part 1, page 4.

it may be observed, that it is sometimes replaced by *o*, as
these vowels have often nearly the same pronunciation;
ex. *moche* vv. 186 a. 191; *dorst* v. 294; *moch* v. 302; *bot*
(but) v. 311; there are also instances, where *u* is written
instead of M. Eng. *o*, ex. *luve* 321; a. o. But the *o* is often
retained: *love* v. 348; *u* is sometimes employed in short
terminations, instead of an ancient *i*, as *nobul* v. 108 (L.
nobilis); instead of A. S. *o: yclepud* v. 119, A. S. *gecly-
pod* M. E. *yclept;* instead of M. E. *i: murþe* v. 186 M. E.
mirth, A.S. *mirð, myrð; furlong* v. 11. *u* is often used,
where M. E. has short *ou: curteysliche* v. 359.

The letters *y* and *i* are used by turns without any
difference; ex. personal pronoun, 1:st pers. *i* and *y. y* is also
used in terminations instead of M. E. *e*, ex. *buschys* ß), a
weakened form of the A. S. termination *-as* v. 19 a. s. o.
— *w* and *u* are also used by turns.

On the use of the consonants, we have already remarked the retaining of some old characters; only a few other
observations may be made.

The Mod. E. *sh* is here generally written *sch* ex. *sche*,
v. 67; *schuld* v. 74, and sometimes the single *ch* is used
ex. *worchipful* v. 113; the *ch* is even employed instead of
c as: *schore* v. 130. — When the vowel has a short sound,
the consonants are in this romance sometimes doubled and
sometimes only a single consonant is employed. As it would
be impossible to give some rules for the employing of vowels
and consonants, because it is too much arbitrary, we will
now finish our observations on this point and begin our
etymological researches on the verbal forms in the romance
of William and the Werwolf, (we refer to the specimen of
this romance, printed by Mr. Morris in his Specimens of
early English; p. 237).

In treating the language in the Romance of William
and the Werwolf, we will at first consider the verbs.

ß) In the Lowland-Scotch dialect most substantives form their plural
by the termination *-is* often written *ys;* ex. *in þai Landys;* Wyntowns
Orygynal Cronykil of Scotland. V. 2, 110; My sensis are Rob. and Mak.
boltis so hair; Holland, The buke of the Howlat, ed. by Laing 60.

Grammatical remarks.

The verbs have, of course, in this romance dropped many old inflections, but, nevertheless, there are to be found many peculiarities, worthy of noticing. The tendency of the strong verbs to pass over into weak forms, [1]) commonly met with in most languages, appears already in the dialect of this romance, ex. *weped*, v. 334, Ag. S. weóp; *welt* vv. 140 a. 219, Angl. S. *weóld*.

The *u* is frequently dropped in the infinitive of the verbs and in the preterite plural, and often even in the present indicative and subjunctive, though it is also some-times retained in the last forms, for instance:

And þus it bi-tide þat time, as *tellen* our bokes v. 5.

Appeles and alle þinges, þat children after *wilnen* v. 59.

Ak now ge þat *arn* hende, haldes ow stille, v. 104.

þei *han* me fostered and fed faire to þis time, v. 232.

The *n* most often is dropped; f. ex.

But carfuli gan sche crie so kenely and lowde,

þat maydenes and migthi men manliche to hire *come*,
150, 151.

And briddes ful bremely on the bowes *singe*, v. 21.

The Northern termination *es* occurs in the 3:d pers. plur. in the following examples:

William, sire, wel y wot, wiges me *calles;* v. 228.

Whanne þou komest to kourt among þe kete lordes,
And knowest alle þe kuþþes þat to kourt *langes;* vv.
319, 320.

...... also greteþ wel oft

Alle mi freyliche felawes, þat to þis forest *longes*, v.v.
348, 349.

The particle *at*, a northern peculiarity, is sometimes employed before the infinitive; ex. at abaie v. 44, but the particle *to* is most often used.

The termination *en* in the infinitive is seldom employ-ed, as for ex.

[1]) In the Lowland-Scotch dialect of these times this transformation from old strong forms to weak ones are much more often met with, than in the Engl. writers during the 14th and 15th centuries.

And wolden *brusten* þe best, nad he be þe liȝttere
v. 152.

But the final - *e* is usually retained; ex. *wayte* v.
146 (= to watch for). Besides the infinitive, there is to be
found a gerund, preceded by the particle *to* and terminating in *ene*; as v. 309 to *done*; v. 325 to *rekene*.

The first person present indicative generally terminates in a vowel, this vowel being *e* as in Angl. S., but it
is sometimes dropped. Ex. y þe praye v. 237.

The second person singular present indic. generally
terminates in — *est*.

Ex. When þou *komest* to court among the kete lords,
And *knowest* alle þe kuþþes þat to kourt langes v.v. 319,320.
Sometimes the northern termination *es* is employed; ex.

And alle oþer frely felawes þat þou faire *knowes* v 355.

Go calle to me þe cowherd þow *clepus* þi fadere v. 238.

The third person sing. present ind. terminates most
frequently in *es*, which is the case in the Northern as well
as in the West-Midland dialect.

Ex. þere pried he in and partiliche *biholdes*
How hertely þe herdes wif hules þat child. v.v. 94, 95.

And as blive, boute bod, he *braydes* to þe quene v. 147.
(M.E. And as quickly, without delay, he rushes to the queen).

But the Southern inflexion *eþ* (= eth) also often
occurs. Ex.

...... so balfully he *ginneþ* v. 82.

»But lelly oþer likenes þat *longeþ* to man-kynne,

But a wild werwolf, ne walt he never after v.v. 141 ,142.

The Anglo S. inflexions *ede, edest, ede,* in the preter.
ind. of weak verbs are often retained in this dialect.

Ex. And *buskede* him out of þe busches etc. v. 19.
»What sone», *seide* þe couherde, »*seidestow* i was here?»
v. 256.

But the final *e* is sometimes dropped, ex. *shewed* v.
186 etc.

The preterite plural of weak verbs has usually the
old inflection *den*, but the *n* is frequently dropped and
only the termination *ede* employed, and sometimes even
the final *e* is dropped.

Ex. So kynde and so corteys comsed he þere,
þat alle ledes him *lovede* þat *loked* on him ones,
And *blesseden* þat him bare and brougt in-to þis worlde,
v.v. 183—185.

The terminations of the imperative may be seen by the
following examples:

»Bi stille barn», quaþ þemperour, — »*blinne* (= cease)
of þi sorwe», v. 311.

And gode sire, for godes love, also *greteþ* wel oft
Alle mi freyliche felawes, ... v.v. 349, 350.

The present participle sometimes ends in the Northern
termination *and* (Angl. S. *ende*), but this termination is
often substituted by the modern *ing*.

Ex. *Clougtand* kyndely his schon, as to here craft
falles, v. 12.
þe cherl, *grocching*, forþ goþ wiþ þe gode child, v. 260.
Hunting v. 193.

We may here remark, that the verbal nouns in -ing
are already used as early as in Lagamon's Brut for the
true part. pres.; the old termination *and* was long retained
in the North. Eng. and in Lowland Scotch, but even in
these dialects the old inflexion gradually lost its ground.

The past participle in this dialect most often omits
the prefix *y* (i), except *yclepud* v. 119 (Mod. E. yclept),
ycharged v. 171, perhaps owing to some influence from the
North of England. The past participle of the strong verbs
sometimes has the old termination *en*, which was retained
in the North. Engl. and which is in Mod. E. usually employed, but in the dialect of William and the Werwolf
the *n* is most often dropped and only the termination *e*
employed, which is a peculiarity for the Midland dialects.

Ex. ...... where forþ þe herde hadde *bore* þan barn
beter is to geme v.v. 88, 89.
þat he ne wist in þis world were þei were bicome, v. 211.
Ac komen was he of kun þat kud was ful nobul, v. 108.

Etymologies.

Now passing over to the etymological treatise of the verbs in » *William and the Werwolf*», we divide them, accor- ding to the newest grammatical systems, in 1. *strong*, 2. *weak*. Those who do not belong to either of these classes may be called 3. *anomalous*. In Angl.-S. there existed *redupli- cating* verbs, as in Icelandic, but as their forms in Middle- E. are corrupted, some of them having passed into weak forms, and the other having nowise retained the reduplica- tion, we do not here consider them as a special class.

The character of the strong conjugation in the old dialect of the romance, here treated, is as in all Teutonic languages the change of vowels in the preterite, and some- times also in the participle past. The tendency of the New-E. verbs to throw off the termination *-en* in past participle occurs already in this ancient dialect, as we have seen by the above given examples. We do not think proper to divide the strong and weak verbs in their sub- divisions, according to Grimm, because the number of them are limited.

1. *Strong verbs.*

v. 333. *Bi-falle*, pret. *bifel* (v.v. 1, 155); Ag.-S. be- feallan, composed by the Ag.-S. prefix *be* and the verb feallan, O.-Sax. fallan, Swed. falla, Germ. fallen, Mod. E. fall, Du. vallen, Mid.-Lat. falliare, L. *pellere*, Sanscr. root *sphal* (to tremble); the Gr. σφάλλειν and its derivatives look, as if the radical meaning of the word were to slip. (Wedgwood).

The English verb is distinguished from that of most other languages by wanting characteristic radical forms. A few exceptions may be remarked. We have the Sax. prefix *be*, as in Mid.-E. bifalle, Eng. befall, generally applied only to verbal and nominal roots, though some- times an adjective is verbalised by the aid of this prefix as to *besot*, to make sottish, which is authorised by Milton and Shakspeare. Moreover there are the Gr. and Fr. en- ding *-ise*, as in *authorise*, the L. *ate*, as in *create* and the

L. and Fr. *fy*, as to *specify*, but these are only employed with Gr., L. and Fr. roots. In this romance we meet with the prefix *of*, as *of-saw* v. 47. The Mod.-E. termination *en*. which is not the sign of the mood as in O.-Eng. may also be mentioned as in blacken, compare the Sw. *na* in *svartna* a. o.

v. 46. *Bihold*, v. 94 biholdes, pret. *biheld* v. 212; Mod.-Eng. *behold*; Ag.-S. *behealdan*, from the simple verb healdan, to regard, observe, which sense is retained in the compound Eng. form. Mr. Wedgwood remarks that the notion of preserving, holding is originally derived from that of looking, which may indeed be seen by many analogies. Moreover Mr. Grimm says upon this circumstance in his »Wörterbuch» 1, 1321: »wie die wörter des sehens übergehen in den begriff des hütens, tueri schützen, unser warten, garder beschirmen ausdrückt, der sehende sein auge auf die gegenstände richtet, sie im auge behält, sie in aufsicht nimmt, so erklärt sich, dass unser behalten im Ag.-S. behealdan, Eng. behold anschauen, anblicken aspicere bedeutet».

v. 53. *Bad*, pret. from Mid. E. bidde, Mod. E. bid (pr. bade, pp. bidden); here the sense of the word is to order something to be done; the translation of the verse being: »bade him cease barking and spoke to the child», in this sense the verb *bid* is derived from Ag. S. beódan, bead, geboden, Germ. *bieten*, Swed. *bjuda* (See Wedgwood). But in the sense of to pray (this sense now obsolete) it is derived from Ag.-S biddan (biddian) bæd, gebeden, Germ. bitten, Swed. bedja.

v. 64. *Bitok*, pret. of *bitake* to hand over, to give, Mod. E. *betake* to apply to; pr. betook pp. betaken, from the simple verb take, O. N. taka, Sw. taga, from the same root as L. tangere, to touch, and the It. attaccare, to fasten one thing to another; O. E. taken, in Orm. takenn (Mueller). Obs. Swed. subs. tåg and tag.

v. 89. *Bore*, an old pp. from the O. E. verb to beren or *bere* pret. bare v. 185; imperat. *bere* v. 321, the pp. *bore* also occurs in v. 229, the *n* being dropped in the Midland dialect of this romance, though it is retained in

Mod. E. This verb is to be found in many languages,
Lat. *ferre*, Gr. φέρειγ, Ag. S. beran, bær, boren, Goth.
bairan, Swed. båra; from the Sanscr. root bhri (Chambers's
Dict.) the vb. bibharmi.

v. 152. *Brusten* (to burst) pret. barst v. 363; the pp.
does not occur in the extract of this romance given by
Mr. Morris; it was in South. E. written ibrosten or ibrusten;
the inf. has here retained the old termination, which is often
dropped in the dialect of this romance. This verb spelled
in Ang. S. berstan, brystan, O. H. G. berstan, Germ.
bersten, Swed. brista, Gael. bris, brisd. (break). The root
appears under the forms brik, bris, brist, brit (Wedgwood).

v. 54. *Come* also written *com* v. 259, pret. *com* (vv. 36,
171, 45 etc.) come v. 151, pp. *come* v. 303, komen v.
108, 276, kome 225, 3:d pers. sing. pres. komes v. 203,
comes v. 6, komest v. 379. The spelling fluctuates between
c and *k*, the latter probably owing to Northern influence
(or perhaps directly derived from the O. S. *kuman*);
from Ag. S. cuman, cviman; Germ. kommen, Sw. komma;
the Ag. S. cviman is probably the original form, the root
being cvim; the qv (= kv, cv) is retained in the Germ.
beqvem, Sw. beqväm; the transition of the vowel *i* to *o*
after a rejected *v* occurs for ex. in Sw. qvinna and kona;
the O. E. *com* has grown up by a contraction *quam*
which is the older form; compare the Sw. kom; came is of
later date. In the Eng. adj. comely and the Du. komelick,
the sense of the verb is convenire, decere, as the Eng.
become.

v. 211. *Bicome*, p.p. of *bicome*, Mod. Eng. *become*,
Ag. S. becuman; see *come*.

v. 136. *Bigat*, pret. form bigete(n) bigat bigotten (to
obtain) from the prefix *bi* (be) and *geten*. The inf. *gete*
v. 329; and pret. *gat* v. 110: Ag. S. *getan*, *gitan*; O. N.
geta, Sw. gitta, especially signifying posse, valere, O. H. G.
gezzan (compare the Sw. förgäta); to *forget* to away get,
to lose one's mental acquisitions (Wedgwood).

v. 164. *Bi-stode* (stood by, stood still) pret. of *bi-*
standen, from Ag. S. *standan* ståd gestanden, O. N. *standa*

stôð standinn, Sw. stå, contracted from O. Sw. stánda; Gr. ἵ-στημι, L. *stare.*

»The root of the word is *stad,* the primary meaning being to strike against, to come to stop». (Wedgwood) Compare Gael. *stad,* stop, Devon. *stat* stopped (Halliwell) Scot. to *stot,* to stop (Jamieson).

v. 340. *Bygan.* Here the prefix is written *by,* the letters y and i being used by turns in this romance, as we have remarked before. The above cited form is preter. of *biginnen,* bigun, bigin; Mod. E. *begin* from a root, which is to be found in all Indo-European languages, signifying, according to Wedgwood, to conceive, to bear young, to know, to be able, the fundamental meaning being to attain to, to acquire. The forms *gan* v.v. 69, 122, 150, 84, 299 and *gun* 279 occur also in this romance and may be considered as auxiliaries, having nearly the same signification as *do,* which use is frequent in O. E. and Sc. for instance.

> To Scotland went he then in hy
> And all the land *gan* occupy.

Barbour.

> Aboutin undern *gan* this Erle alight.

Clerk of Oxford's tale.

40. *Drow* and v. 42 *drawe* are preterite forms of drawen drow drawe (or idrawen) in the Midland dialect, Mod. E. *draw* and *drag,* from Ag. S. *dragan.* L. trahere, Sw. draga, Germ. tragen. The Ag. S. guttural has here changed to *w* as is often the case at the end of words and between two vowels in English; ex. Ag. S. hagaþorn, Eng. hawthorn.

v. 12. *Falles* (and v. 328) pres., *fel* v.v. 85, 192, pret. from the Middle Eng. vb. fallen fel ifallen. See bi-falle.

v. 62. *Finde* inf.; findes v. 93, 3d pers. sing. pres., findestow the second pers. sing. (this contraction of the verb with the second pers. pronoun is often to be found in O. E.) pret. fond (v.v. 71, 81, 88 282); there exists also the form *founde* in pret. plur., where the e is retained from the ending *en.* The part. past does not occur in this romance but it was probably written *fonden* or fonde in the Midland dialect. The word is derived from Ag. S. *findan* (ire investigare, invenire) Goth. *finþan,* Germ. finden, O. N. and

Sw. finnä (where *d* is assimilated). As a comparison with Ag. S., we here represent the flexion of the Midland, pret. form of finde.

Midl. Eng.		Ag. S.	
fond	fonde (founde)	fand	fundon
fonde	fonde	funde	fundon
fond	fonde	fand	fundon

v, 247. *gif*, 3:d pers. sing. pres. subj. and *gaf* v. 110 pret. of the vb. *give* gaf given, Mod. E. give gave given from the Ag. S. gifan, Goth. giban, O. N. gefa, Sw. gifvu. Wedgwood mentions its relation with the Gael. gabh, take, lay hold of, seize; and consequently gives the original sense of give = to cause another to take.

v. 56. *Hiat* (promised) is a preterite sprung out from the Ag. S. pret. *hêht, hêt, het* (Rask) of the strong vb. hâtan, (het hâten E. Müller, to promise). There is in Middle Eng. a strong vb. hote (to command, name) pret. hight, p.p. boten (ihoten), even the p.p. hat, batte, from Ag. S. hâtan (pr. hatte p.p. gehaten) to call. name; from hence the pret. form *hiat* v. 68); the fundamental signification of the root of these words is anything hot, burnt; compare Sw. *heta* and subst. hetta, Germ. heissen and Hitze. The past participles of the O E. vb. *hote* are employed for ex. in »Genesis and Exodus» v. 237 »He is gungest, *hoten* benia-min»; Kyng Alisaunder v. 4862 »There is another ydle [1] *halt* [2] Gangerides.».

The »g» in *hight* has according to Latham been used only by analogy with the words high, height.

The two preterits may probably have sprung out from the strong Ag. S. preterit heht, as E. Müller thinks.

v. 251. *Help*, subj. 3:d pers. sing.; the same form occurs in v.v. 265, 276; the verb is written in inf. helpen or helpe, pret. halp (holp) p.p. iholpen in the South. dialect. In the Ormulum the subj. of this vb. is written *helpe* with *e* as in Ag. S. Ag. S. helpan, Goth. hilpan, O.-N. hjâlpa, Sw. hjelpa, Germ. helfen. Weigand says in his Dictionary

[1] Island.
[2] An error for *hatte* (Morris).

1,496 »das wort stimmt lautverschoben zu Litth. gebeti
helfen, retten, und führt, da sein ableitend erscheint, auf
die urwurzel hilan».

v. 337. *Heve* (to raise up); this is the only form of
this verb, which is found in Morris' extract of the romance
of W. and the Werwolf. The verb had in the old South.
Eng. dialect the form hebben, haf (hof), iboven; M. E.
heave, from A. S. hebban, O. N. hefia, Germ. heben, Sw.
hâfva. The form heve is more modernized than the old
S. E. hebben.

v. 269. *Knowe* (inf. with rejected *n*) i know v. 234;
there are two forms of the second pers. sing. pres. ind., viz.
knowest (with Southern inflexion) v. 320 and *knowes*, with
the ending *es*, which is peculiar for the Northern dialect,
but which is also very often employed in the West Midland
dialect of Shropshire; the preter. *knew* v.v. 144, 297. (p.p.
in the South. dial. iknowen). There exists also an O. E.
form knawen, from Ag. S. cnâwan, L. gnoscere (noscere)
Gr. γνῶναι; the original root is by Wedgwood supposed to
be gen or ken, signifying probably to seize, apprehend;
perhaps identical with the root of can, kin (E. Müller).

v.v. 18, 58. *Lay* preter. from lie, lay, lain (lien in
the Bible); O. S. E. legen leig ilogen; derived from Ag. S.
licgan, liggan, ligêan, O. N. liggia, Sw. ligga; akin to Lat.
legere, to lay; as appears from colligere, to lay together;
Gr. λέγειν (orig. to lay), λέγεσθαι (to lie), λέχος, a couch,
bed (Wedgwood).

v. 357. *Nam* (took), pret. of the O. E. vb. *neme* or
nime nam inomen, from the Ag. S. *niman*, Germ. nehmen,
O. N. nema, Mod. E. to nim, Sw. nimma (in compounds);
Wedg. and Rapp suppose the Lat. emere (to bay) to be
identical with the vb. nime; the stem seems to be iman,
where the *n* may be derived from a compound with a
particle, according to Schwenck (compare Germ. neben,
from eben).

v. 240 *Quaþ* (and vv. 266, 311, 315), only once (v.
241) the form quoþ occurs; preterites from the old verb
queþen or quethe, derived from Ag. S. cwêdan (to say) Goth
qviþan; the original signification of this word is, according

to Wedgwood, to dabble in water, from whence the signification of idle talking is often taken; this sound is also often applied to the chattering of birds; thus we have for example Sw. qvåda (to sing), qvida (to lament), qvittra (to twitter); Germ. quatscheln (to dabble), quatschen (to chatter); the compound verb bequeathe, Ag.-S. becwédan, exists still in Mod E., but from the O. E. vb quethe only the preterite quoth remains, even this being rather obsolete. The O. E. quaþ quite corresponds with the Sw. quad (sang).

v. 39. *Ros*, pret. of the verb rise ros (ras) risen, Mod. E. rise rose risen, from Ag.-S. rîsan, O. N. rîsa, Ag.-S. reosan, to rush, to fall O. H. G. risan, to fall; the original meaning of the word seems to have been the rustling sounds of fragments falling to the ground; compare Sw. rassla; as the compound verb, signifying to fall is wanting in Engl., the simple verb has got the signification of falling in the opposite direction.

v. 208. *Renne* inf.; pret. ran v. 39; the inf. is also spelled *ren* in O. E., O. N. renna Ag.-S. rinnan and, transposed, yrnan, pr. arn pl. urnon, pp. urnen; in the Mod. E. run the obscure vowel of the Ag. S. preterite has found its way even into the other forms.

v. 341. *Ride*, he rides v. 196, pret. rod v. 189; Mod. E. ride, rode ridden, A. S. ridan, Sw. rida (to be carried on horseback), O. N. riða, to be borne on a horse or in a ship; the original meaning of the verb is probably the same as that of rise, namely to come down, then to be borne along.

v. 17. *Speke* (vv. 77, 254, 259), by Ormulum spekenn, Mod. E. speak spoke spoken, O. South. E. speken spok (spak) ispeken, ispoken; the preter. spak is common in the Northern dialect; so for ex. Walter Scott says that King James 1 of England »spak braid Scotch«; the vb. is derived from Ag.-S. spécan, sprécan, spreocan; Germ. sprechen; parallel forms with and without a liquid after the initial *s* are to be found in many languages. Wedgwood derives the word from Low Germ. spaken, to crack from drought; but more probable seems the derivation of Mr. Schwenck; from a root sprik as a parallel form of brik (Germ. brechen) in analogy with the Sw. spricka (to burst asunder), spricka ut, (to break out).

v. 21. *Singe*, 3:d pers. plur. pres. ind. with rejected *n*; in South Eng. singen, sang (song) isungen (isongen), Mod. E., sing, sang (sung), sung; Ag. S. singan, Goth. *siggvan*, O. N. sangra (to murmur); probably from the sound.

v. 212. *Se* inf.; pret. seiᵹ v. 32, say v. 217, seye v. 24, sawe v. 215, past p. seie v. 268; the preterite is sometimes spelled seᵹ in South. E. As to the change of the O. E. letter ᵹ in the preterite of this verb to the Mod. E. *y*, it may be observed that many words are in Mod. E. spelled with y, where O. E. and Middl. E. had »ᵹ», for ex. ᵹet v. 266, E. yet; ᵹa v. 247, E. yea; South. Eng. saᵹ (saw) Midl. E. say, a. s. o. The Midl. E. *se*, Mod. E. *see*, O. E. sen, seon are derived from Ag.-S. seón, Goth. saihvan, O. N. siâ, Sw. sc.

v. 10. *Sat*, pret. of the verb sit, South. E. siten sat iseten, Mod. E. sit from Ag.-S. sittan, L. sed-ere, Gr. ἕζ-ομαι, from a root spread out over all Indo-Eur. languages.

v. 124. *Schapen*, p. p. of the old vb. schapen schop (schup) (i) schapen (ischopen); a weak form also occurs in pp. schaped vv. 139, 143, which is the common flexion in Mod. E; but in the Bible we meet with the old form shapen. The word is derived from Ag.-S scapan, sceapan, pr. scóp pp. scapen, sceapen, O. N., Sw. skapa, O. H. G. scapan; the original meaning uncertain; according to Wedgwood probably from the notion of carving or shaping with the knife.

v. 257. *Swor*, pret. of the old vb. swere swor, sworen; Mod. E. swear swore sworn, from Ag.-S. swerian, p. swor, pp. gesworen; Sv. svâra, svârja.

v. 368. *Sleie*, pp. of (sle sloᵹ) sleie, Mod. E. slay slew slain from Ag.-S. slean sloh geslagen, Goth. slahan, O. N. slâ (contr. from slaha) Germ. schlagen, Sw. slâ to slay, slaga (an instrument); the word is formed from the sound.

v. 201. *Takes*, 3:d pers. sing. of the vb. take, pr. tok (v. 60) pp. take (v. 131). As to the derivation see »bi-tok» v. 64. Ag.-S. tacan, tok we tócon, tacen. As to the forms of the preter. Ag.-S. tok, tócon, Middl. E. tok, Mod. E. took, we remark that this transition of the Ag.-S. ó is very common; compare Ag.-S. dóm, Midd. E. dome on dom Mod. E. doom; Ag.-S. móna, Midd. E. mone, Mod. E. moon.

v. 122. *Wexe* pret. wax (v. 34) wex (vv. 138, 355) pp. wox (with rejected *en*), Mod. E. to wax, Ag.-S. weaxan, p. weóx, wox, pp. weaxen geweaxen (Bosworth), O. N. vaxa, Sw. växa, N. H. G. wachsen, akin to the Gr. αὔξω.

v. 92. W*inne*, inf. with rejected *n*, pr. wan v. 179, pp. wonne (with rejected *n*); Mod. E. win won won; Ag.-S. winnan (to struggle), O. N. vinna (to get) Ag.-S. gewinnan (to gain); Ag.-S. subst. win, wine (labour).

v. 181. *With-hold* and the simple vb. *hold* v. 33, imper. haldes (ow = you) v. 104 hald, sec. pers. sing. imper. v. 332. from the vb. hold held holden, the last form now obsolete and replaced by *held*. Ag.-S. *healdan, Germ. halten*.

v. 310. ꝺelde to requite and v. 308 ꝺeld; 3:d pers. sing. pres. ꝺeldes v. 223, the vb ran in O. South. E. ꝺelden ꝺald (ꝺold, ꝺeld) iꝺolden, Mod. Eng. yield; in Orm. yeldenn, Ag.-S. gildan, gyldan, geldan, O. N. gjalda, Sw. gälda, gälla.

2. *Weak verbs.*

v. 44. *Abaye* (to bark) Morris: = »at bay», but that is very improbable, as the verse runs: and evere þe dogge at þe hole held it *at abaye*. I think it may be derived directly from O. Fr. a(b)bayer (Wedgwood), aboyer It. abbaiare (Gr. βαύζειν), S. ad-baubari in Lucret.; the simple form *baie* (M. E. bay) occurs v. 33.

v. 54. *Acoyed* (enticed) pret. of *acoye;* from Du. koye kooi (cage), vogel-kooi, a bird-cage (Mueller).

vv. 67, 224. *Ask* from Ag.-S. ácsian, áscian (to seek), Sw. åska, Germ. heischen, Gael. aisk (a request).

v. 68. *Answe.·* from Ag.-S. andswarjan, answarjan; swarjan = affirmare, respondere (Ettmüller) Ag.-S. swaran (to answer) swerian (to swear).

v. 137. *Anoynted*, pp. from *anoynt*, M. E. anoint, Fr. oindre, part. oint, Lat. unct-us from unguere.

v. 148. *Astrangeled*, pp. of the vb *astrangele*, Mod. E. strangle, O. Fr. estrangler, N. Fr. étrangler Lat. strangulare from the Gr. στραγγαλίζειν (E. Mueller) στράγγειν (to draw tight (Chambers's Dict.)

v. 194. *Attele*, to endeavour; Sc. ettle, N. Prov. E. ettle, attle O. N. ætla, to intend (Morris).

v. 50. *Agreþed* (adorned) pp. of the old verb agreþe, also spelled *agrayde*, (from Ang. Norman origin) to arrange, decorate. Ex.

»Thyn halle *agrayde*, and hele the walle
With clodes and wyth ryche palles.» Laufal, 904.

v. 255. *Agreved*, pp. of agreve, the simple E. vb grieve (to cause pain of mind), subst. *grief*, It greve, from L. gravis.

v. 43. *Awede* (to go mad) from Ag.-S. wédan (to raye, to be mad). Ex.

»He rod agayn as tyd,
And Lybœus so he smyt,
As man that wold *awede*.» Lyb. Discon., 1. 957 (cited
by Wright).

v. 299. *Awondered*, pp. of awonder, v. 36 wondered, a. v. 52 wondred, Ag.-S. wundrjan (Ettmüller), M. E. wonder, Sw. under, undra, Germ. wundern. Schwench derives the word from Germ. winden.

v. 5. *Bi-tide*, *bytidde* v. 30 *bitidde* v. 46, preter. forms of the vb. bitide, Mod. E. betide; from the prefix be and Ag.-S. *tidan* (befall), subst. *tid* (tide, time), S. tid.

v. 9. *Bayte* on (to set on), subst. *bait*, a bull, O N. *beita*, to bait, hunt hawk or dog, O. Fr. *abetter*, to incite, from Ag.-S. *baetan* O. H. G. beizan (zügeln); the word is originally derived from Ag.-S. bîtan, by means of the pret. bât. (Mueller).

v. 14. *Behoued*, pret. of *behoue*, behove, from Ag.-S. behofjan Sw. höfvas, to become, befit; radically connected with the verb to have (Wedgwood).

v. 19. *Buskede* and busked v. 361, pret. of the vb. buske, M. E. busk (to prepare) according to Wedgwood from O. N. buask, for *bua* sik (induere vestes); »They *busked* and maked them boun.» Sir Tristram.

v. 14. *Blowed*, pret. of *blow* (florere); in Mod. E. this verb is strong and its pp. is blown; from Ag.-S. blôwan, bleów, blôwen (E. Mueller), Ag.-S. weak blôwian blówode geblówod (Bosworth). Bosworth in his compendious Angl.-S. Dictionary does not give the strong form at all. The primary sense is (according to Wedgwood) to shine. to exhibit bright colours, to glow. Compare Eng. blowze, a red-cheeked girl, gho has been running abroad in the wind.

v. 33. *Berke*, pret. berkyd v. 46, Mod. E. *bark* Ag.-S. beorcan, borcjan, from an imitation of the sound; O. N. barki, the throat. As to the spelling, it may be observed that *e* and *a* before *r* in a long syllable has sometimes the same sound; compare M. E. clerk, serjeant etc. O. E. Darby. M. E. Derby.

v. 53. *Blinne*, imp. blinne v. 311; blinnen; Morris. Extr. of Genesis and Exodus, v. 57. As Mr. Morris does not mention the verb in his list of the O. E. strong vbs, we have placed it here among the weak vbs; Ag.-S. blinnan blan, blunnen from *bi* (= be) and Ag.-S. linnan (to cease) Prov. E. *lin;* Sc. leen, O. N. linna; O. H. G. bilinnen,

v. 73. *Brougt* (vv. 78, 105, 185) irreg. pret. of the vb. bring (vv. 132, 164), Sw. bringa, Ag.-S. bringan and in all Teutonic languages except in O. N.; the pret. is formed of another stem than the inf.; comp. Sw. bragte, Germ. brachte; it is related to the Ag.-S. béran Gr. φέρειν and E. break, Ag.-S. brĕcan (Mueller).

v. 147. *Braydes*, 3:d pers. sing. pres. of *brayde* (to start, to rush to), from Ag.-S. *bredan, bregdan*, to weave, braid, drive; O. N. bregða, to change, to awake out of sleep, start; the original meaning is probably to go hither and thither (hin and her ziehen, Mueller); O. E. *at a braid*, at once; Shakspeare uses braid for manners:

Since Frenchmen are so *braid*,

Marry who will, I'll live and die a maid

Comp. O. N. *at braga*, to imitate.

v. 162. *Buschen* (to busk, to go out). See *buskede* v. 19.

v. 185. *Blesseden*, 3:d pers. plur. pret. with the old ending, from the vb. blessen, M. E. bless from Ag.-S. *bletsjan*, to bless, to consecrate, which is to be derived from

Ag.-S. bliðe, Eng. blithe, Goth. bleiþs, Sw. blid (Wedgwood).

v. 96. *Baþede*, 3:d pers. sing. pr. of baþe, M. E. bathe, Ag.-S. baðjan, Sw. bada, Germ. baden Sw. badda to warm, to burn; Mueller indicates the origin to be in the Sanscr. root bâd, vâd (lavare), Gr. βαθὺς deep, βάπτειν emerge, Wedgwood thinks the Sw. baka to be another form of the same word by the intermedium of Germ. bähen, to warm. The explanation of Mueller seems to be more preferable.

v. 195. *Bruttenet* (cut in pieces), pp. of Ag.-S brytan (to break); bryttjan (to crumble); brytlic. broken in pieces; whence E. brittle; In the North of E. and in Sc. brickle, brockle, bruckle, are used in the sense of brittle, break. (See buast v. 152).

v. 339. *Bikenned* (v. 360) (= commended) 3:d pers. sing. pr. of the vb. bikennen, from bi (= be) and Ag.-S. cennan to know, (to vouch the truth); Sw. bekänna, Germ. bekennen, Sc. ken.

v. 343. *Beseche*, 1:st pers. pres. sing. of the vb. beseche even written beseke, besech, M. E. beseech, Ag.-S., bisêcan. Chaucer employs the form beseke f. ex.

»His heart is hard that will not meke
When men of mekeness him beseke»,

v. 12. *Clougtand* (patching) Ag.-S. clût (a patch) *clûtjan* (consuere, clavare, Ettmüller), Du. klotsen (to strike); related to the Fr. *clou*, nail (from L. clavus), vb clouter; the primary sense is uncertain. As to the termination -*and* in the participle clougtand, this ending was grown obsolete in the Southern and Midland dialects already towards the end of the fourteenth century. The transition commenced in the South. dialect before 1300, and the pres. partic. began assuming the form of the verbal noun in -*inge(-ing)*. The ending -*and* (ande) is a Northern peculiarity, and in the dialect North of the Humber, it kept its ground through the 15:th and 16:th centuries, which is evident by its appearing in Scotch works during these centuries. In the Southern dialect the old ending was -*inde*, in the Midland -*ende* (-end). The Ag.-S. partic. ending in -*ende* is nevertheless not corrupted into -*ing*, for such a corruption cannot be defended by analogies in the Engl. language. We think then, according to Max Müller, that the Mod. Eng. partic. in -*ing* is derived from an old locative of a verbal noun in analogy with the dialectical forms a -going, a-thinking a. o. *).

v. 35. *Comsed* (a. v. 183, 277) pret. of the vb *comse* or *comsen*, Mod. E. commence, Fr. commencer, It. cominciare, from L. com (cum) and *initiare*.

v. 54. *Clepud* (vv. 249, 263) pret.; pp. *yclepud* v. 119; þou clepus, 2:d pers. sing. pres. ind. with the peculiar Midland ending (us for u *es)*; Ag.-S. cleopjan, clipjan, clypjan, O. E. clepen, Sc. clep (to tattle); Chaucer uses clappe (to boast); Du kleppen (sonare), klappen, to clap, crack, probably from the sound. The part. yclept is not yet quite out of use and is the last participle, which has preserved the prefix.

v. 61. *Clipped* (embraced) pr. of the vb. *clippe*, Mod E. *clip*, from Ag. S. clyppan (to embrace); O. N. *klippa* Du. klippen (to cut) clip is related to clap by the »Ablaut»; the word is taken, according to Wedgwood, »from an imitation of the snapping noise made by the two blades of the shears».

v. 76. *Chaunge*, Fr. *changer*, M. E. change; the transition of Fr. *a* into *au* was common before an other consonant during the Middle Engl. period; it occurs still in Shakspeare, as auncient for ancient. In Mod. E. it seldom occurs, f. ex. launch for lanch, aunt, O. Fr. ante.

v. 35. *Crye* and v. 150 *crie*, from the sound; Fr. crier, L. *quiritare*, A. S. grætan.

v. 171. *Ycharged* (with retained prefix) pp. of charge. Fr. charger, from L. carrus (a wagon).

v. 206. *Carped*, pret, of carpe (to talk)
»So gone they forthe, *carpende* fast
On this, on that.» Gower in Way.
Mueller derives the word from L. carpere (to pick).
Wedgwood perhaps more right, from Port. carpire (to cry or weep).

*) See Max Müller; Vorlesungen über die Wissenschaft der Sprache, für das Deutsche Publikum bearbeitet v. Böttger; II. p. 13.

Carpyn or talkyn, fabulor, garrulo Ph. Pm.

(Wedgwood),

v. 205. *Chased*, pret. of *chase*, Fr. chasser, It. cacciare from L. part. captus, with the suffix. *iare* (Diez).

v. 342. *Cacc(h)es*, pres. of *cacche*, Mod. E. *catch*, which verb is only a different version of the same word, as chase. but from another French dialect, Picardie, where the word is called *cacher*.

v. 238. *Calle*, imper. and v. 228 *calles*, 3:d pers. plur. pres. of the vb. *calle*, Mod. E. call, Ag. S. ceallian, O. N. kalla, L. calare, Gr. καλεῖν: probably from the sound of one hallooing (Wedgw.).

v. 272. *Coniure*, pres. of the vb. coniure (conjure), from L. con and jurare.

v. 272. *Comande*, pret. commandede v. 336, komanded v. 225; Fr. commander, from the L. con, *manus* and *dare*.

v. 49. *Cloþed* (v. 282), pp. of *cloþe*; from Ag. S. cláð (covering), clæð (a garment), O. N. klædi Sw. klåde, vb. klåda, related to L. claudere, to shut.

v. 49. *Chastised*, pret. of the vb. chastise, Fr. châtier, Lat. castigare.

v. 369. *Comforted*, pp. of comfort, Fr. comforter from L. cum and fortis.

v. 15. *Darked* (was hiding); the word dark is by Morris compared with O. E. *dare* (to lie motionless), used by Chaucer; Low Germ. be-daren to be still; Prov. E. *dor* to frighten, dor a fool (comp. Lw. dåra, darra).

v. 86. *Devise* (to tell, describe) Fr. deviser, It. divisare, L. dividere, divisum divisare, (Mueller).

v. 111. *Deyde*, pret. of *deye*, Mod. E. die; in Ag. S. this vb. is not to be found; only the subst, deàd, deàð occur; O. N. deya, Sw. dö, Sc. dee Goth. divan; there is in Ag. S. a transit. vb. dydan (to kill).

v. 149. *Digt* (v. 304) pp. of the vb. *digte, dighte*, Ag. S. dihtan, Sw. dikta, Germ. dichten from L. dictare (to dictato); Ag. S. diht (a disposing).

v. 149. *Deme* (to judge), M. E. deem, Ag. S. *dêman* (to judge), vowel-changed forms of doom, Sw. dom, döma.

v. 194. *Entred*, preter. of entre, Mod. E. enter (with transposition of *e*), Fr. entrer, from L. intrare.

v. 261. *Ettleden* (arrived) pret. of *ettle*, see *attele* v. 194.

v. 28. *Ferde* (fared) from Ag.-S. féran (pret. ferde) to go; Ag.-S. *ferd* an expedition. M. E. *fare*; Ag.-S. faran, O. N., Sw. fara, Germ. fahren.

v. 31. *Feld*, preter. of the vb. *felen*, Mod. E. feel, Ag.-S. félan, Germ. fühlen, Dan föle, O. N. fjalla (to touch with the palm of the hand); Mueller thinks the O. N. fala (petere) to be the original verb. Compare L. palma, palpare.

v. 178. *Folwe*; pres. fulwes v. 31; preter. folwd. v. 206; the *w* here seems to have sounded as a vowel; concerning the use of o and u by turns, we have many examples that these related vowels are used indifferently in the transition period; Ag.-S. folgjan and *fyligan*; Mod. E. follow, Germ. folgen, Sw. följa, O. N. *fylgja*.

v. 85. *Fret*, preter. (with rejected *te*, as is very common, when the root of the vb. ends in *t*, especially if the *t* is doubled; the verbs terminating in *d* doubled follow the same rule) from the vb. frete freten, Ag.-S. *fretan* (pr. fræt, pp. gefreten) whence Eng. fret (to rub, wear, consume), Eng. fritters, shivers, fragments, Sw. fråta (to corrode, to prey upon); Germ. fressen.

vv. 96, 174 *Fedde*, pret., pp. *fed* (v. 285, 307), pret. with the mediate e dropped; from the vb. feed, Sw. föda, Ag.-S. fédan (alere); Goth, fôdjan; Grimm supposes the existence of and old strong vb. *fadan*, from which the other forms might be explained.

v. 120. *Fostered* (vv. 232, 285, 307, 345), pp. of the verb foster, Ag.-S. *fôstrian*, fôster Ettm., O. N. fôstra, Sw. fostra, from Goth. fôdjan; see above!

v. 55. *Foded*, instead of *fonded* (entised), pret. of the vb. *fonde*, from Ag.-S. fandjan (according to E. Mueller); Compare Ag.-S. fandere, the tempter, Dan. fanden, the devil (Wedgwood).

v. 153. *Fled*, pret. of flee with shortened vowel as in shoe, shod (Compare Sw. fly, flydd, sko skodd) Ag.-S. fleohan, contracted fleon, akin tho fly; both from a root

3

flug, from which also the Lat. fugere is formed by the very common loss of the *e* (Wedgwood).

v. 180. *Feþered*, Mod. E. feathered, from the subst. feather, Ag.-S. fyðer, Sw. fjäder, O. N. fjöðr, Gr. πτερόν, wing; Wedgwood derives the word from Du *vledern* to flap; but, compared with πτερόν (= πετερόν) from πέτειν, πέτεσθαι to fly, the word seems more probably to be derived from the root pat (which in Sscr is = to fly).

v. 182. *Feffed* (endowed), pp. of *feffe* (bestow), from O. Fr. *fieffer*, to convey the *fief* or *fee* (Mid. L. fedum) to a new owner (Morris).

v. 239. *Frayne* (to ask), pret. (frainde or) freinde »Genesis and Exodus» in Morris' extract l. 105 »He herd hem murnen (.) he hem *freinde* for quat». The Ag.-S. fregnan (to enquire) was a strong verb; pret. frægn, pp. frugnen; so was also the O. N. fregna; the *n* does not belong to the root, which is evident by the O. N. pret frâ (inst. of frag) and the Sw. inf. frâga, Germ. fragen. Comp. L. precari, to pray; poscere for porscere (corrupted of proscere).

v. 25. *Gadere*, Ag.-S. *gaderian*, M. E. gather, Du. gaderen (to draw to a heap), Germ. gattern, gatten, from a lost verbal root gidan (Grimm) Ag.-S. to gädere, simul, Eng. together. Comp. Sw. (samman)gadda.

v. 58. *Glosed*, pret. of *glose*, Mod. E. gloss (explain) from Gr. γλῶσσα (tongue).

v. 82. *Ginneþ*, 3:d pers. pres. with the Southern ending þ (th); in the West. Midl. dialect the ending *es* is most often used; in the Southern dialect the old termination eþ (eth) was longer retained; it is generally used by Chaucer and other secular writers, contemporary with Wycliffe and by these also frequently in all persons of the plural, but Wycliffe only employs *th* for the singular. The old vb. *ginne* may probably be derived from Ag.-S. *ginan* to open, to *yawn*, O. N. gîna and ginungagap, O. H. G. geinôn, Gr. χαίνειν.

v. 260. *Grocching*, grumbling; probably from the sound of a person out of temper.

v. 295. *Graunted*, pret. of the vb. *graunte*, Mod. E.

grant; concerning the spelling, see *chaunge* v. 76; the word is according to Diez derived from the L. partic. credens (credent-is).

v. 340. *Glade*, to become glad, to gladden; Ag.-S. *gladian*, to be glad; adj. glæd,, Eng. glad, O. N. glaðr, Sw. glad; akin to Sw. and Germ. glatt; »connected with a numerous class of words founded on the notion of shining» (Wedgw.)

v. 222. *Gretes* (pres.), grette (preter. with shortened vowel as in Ag.-S.) v. 358, *greteþ* 2:d p. imperat.. plur. of the vb. *grete* (salute), Mod. E. greet, Ag.-S. *grétan* (to go to meet) pret. grette, Du. groeten, Germ. grüssen; akin to Ag.-S. grætan, greótan (to cry) Sw. gråta O. E. and dial. grete (cry) (Müller).

v. 56 a. o. *Have*; sec. pers. pres. sing. hast v. 287; 3:d pers. pl. *han* (vv. 232, 307, 310, 350); 3:d pers. sing. haþ 345; pret. hadde (v. 87 a. o.) contr. from havede, which form occurs in the Soutern dialect; had v. 80 (a. o.) hade v. 62), nadde v. 117 instead of n'adde, contracted from the Ag.-S. particle *ne** (not) and hadde; such contractions often occur in old English writers; we have here nad v. 152; *not* = ne wot, v. 309; even *nil*, ne will, *nolde* for ne wolde, *nere* for ne were are to be found. O. N. hafa, Germ. haben, Ag.-S. habban, and even in the Romance langu. Sp. haber, Fr. avoir, L. habere.

v. 95. *Hules*, protects; neither Mueller nor Wedgw. nor Chambers give the word; Ag.-S. *hule* (husk as of corn) from Ag.-S. hilan, hélan; Lat. cel-are, Gr. καλύπτειν; O. E. hele (to conceal) (Halliwell).

v. 148. *Hent*, pret. of hende (to seize), O. N. henda (to seize, happen) Sw. hånda, to happen; Ag.-S. hentan, Goth. *hinþan* (Compare L. pre-hendere).

v. 189. *Hunte*, part. huntyng v. 193; Ag.-S. huntian (venari) Goth. *hinþan* from the »Ablaut» of which it sprung

---

* We often find two negatives combined for strengthening the negative power f. ex. "Nede nadde ghe namore of nigromauncy to lere" v. 117.

out (Mueller). Others compare the word with hound, Gr. κύων (κυν-ός).

202. *Herken*, Mod. E. hearken, harken, hark signifie origin. a low whispering sound: parallel forms to hear Sw. hŏra, O. N. heyra Germ. hŏren.

v. 235. *Herd*, pp. of heren, Mod. E. hear; see above.

v. 245. *Hope* (v. 312) originally to look out for, to expect, Germ. hoffen, Sw. hoppas; Ag.-S. hopjan.

v. 310. *Kyd* (appeared) pp. of the verb kyþe (to shew) Ag.-S. cŷðan, to make known (Morris). There is another form kudde, (revealed, manifested) v. 220, pp. kud v. 312.

v. 45. *Koured*, pr. of koure, Mod. E. cower (with the common transposition of *e*), lit. to sit in a corner, W. cwrian, cwr, corner; Gael, *curr* a corner, pit. Compare O. N. hruka, a heap.

v. 61. *Kest.* pret. (of a vb. *kesse* instead) of kiss Ag.-S. cyssan Sw. kyssa, Goth kukjan; akin to O. N. kok, throat.

vv. 12, 64. *Kepe*, pret. *kepud* (v. 3), the *ud* being a remain of the Ag.-S. ending *ode;* keped vv. 160, 176, 188 kept v. 206 Mod. E. keep. from Ag.-S. cepan, to observe, Sot. kepe care, Du kepen.

v. 67. *Kolled* pret. of kolle embrace; probably akin to M. E. collar.

v. 126. *Kuvere*, M. E. *recover*, Fr. recouvrer from L. *re-cuperare*.

v. 241. *Krowned* M. E. crowned, pp. of crown from Gr. χορώνη, crown.

v. 332. *Kenned* (taught, shown) Ag.-S. cennan, Sw. kānna, Sc. ken (with Burns) Germ. kennen; from the same root as *can, con know* (Mueller).

v. 362. *Kayred* (went) Ag.-S. cyrran, cérran, cŷran (to turn); Germ. kehren.

Ligt, Mod. E. *lighten*, Ag.-S. *lihtan* lihtian to, shine; subst. E. light, Germ. Licht.

v. 81. *Leved* (remained) pr. 200 lefte pp. of *leve*, Mod. E. leave, Ag.-S. læfan, O. N. leifa Sw. lemna. Compare Gr. λείπειν, L. linquere

v. 20. *Lent* (gave) pret. of lene, v. 316 lene pres. subj. Mod. E. lend, Ag.-S. lænan, commodare, Sw. lâna, Germ. ehnen; Ag.-S. llhan O. N. leigja, Sw. lega.

v. 23, *Lorked*, pret. of lorke, Mod. E. lurk, to lie in wait, *lurch* to roll suddenly to one side (as a ship) to filch; akin to Sw. lura, even to lirka, lurka (Wedgw.); lurk and lurch are, by Mahn, derived from W. *llerch*, a frisk, llercian, to lurk, to frisk about.

vv. 26, 102. *Liked*, pret. of like, O. N. líka Ag.-S. lícjan, according to Bopp from Goth. ga-leiks by omitting the prefix.

v. 29. *Layked* (playd) pret. of *layke*, even spelled leyke: »The Story of Havelok the Dane» l. 131 »Also he wold (e) with him *leyke*»; from Ag.-S. lácan to play, lác play; Vulg. E. *lark* Sw. leka, lek.

v. 29. *Lesten* (where the wowel *i* has weakened to *e*) listenes 159 from Ag.-S. *hlystan*, gehlystan hlistan, O. N. hlustu ausculture, hlyða, Sw. lyda, lyssna Gr. κλύειν, L. cluere from the Sanscr. root çru O. N. hlust, W. clust, an ear.

v. 141. *Longeþ*, 3:d pers. sing. pres. and *longes*, 3:d pers plur.with changed vowel and with the Northern termination, *longes*, 3:d pers. pl. v. 349, *longed* v. 71 pret. of the vb. *longe* Mod. E. belong Du langen, Vulg. Sw. anbelanga, Germ. belangen, to concern.

v. 100. *Loked* (and 184, 209) pr. of loke, Mod. E. look Ag.-S. lócjan; akin to L. lucere; O. N. *glugga* (o spy), gluggr, Sw. *glugg* (hole). Compare also Sw. lucka.

v. 115. *Lerned*, pp. of lernen Mod. E. learn Ag.-S. leornjan; the *n* does not belong to the root, which is evident from the other forms: to *lere* (= learn) v. 117, pr. lerde (= taugt) v. 330 Ag.-S. læran Sw. lära, Sc. lare (each).

v. 321. *Luve*, first pers. pres., lovest v, 273 pret. lovede v. 184; Sc. luve Ag.S-. lufjan leofjan, Germ. lieben, Goth liubs; compare L. libet; Sansc. lubh (o desire).

v. 279. *Lye*, Mod. E. lie, Ag.-S. leógan, Goth. liugan, Sw. ljuga, Germ. lügen; Gael leog (idle tak).

v. 156. *Maked*, pp. mak v. 356 (pres. subj.), made (v. 22, 134) contracted from makede, inf. make, Germ. machen, Sw. maka, O. H. G. mahhôn (to connect Ag.-S. macian; akin to Goth. magan (to be great) and mag, root of L. magnus (Chambers) Grimm. says that the word seems to be related to L. macte and a vb. magere, from the above mentioned root mag.

v. 82. *Missed* pret. of misse, Ag.-S. missjan, O. N. missa (to lose) Sw. mista, Du missen.

v. 196. *Marked*, pret. of mark, Ag.-S. *mearcjan*, Goth. *marka*, boundary, Sw. märka, abst. märke; the word may also have taken influence from Fr. marque, It. Sp. marca.

v. 267. *Negh* (to came near) Mod. E. adv. nigh (near) Ag.-S. neáh, nêh, nih, O. N. nâ, Germ. nahe (compare Engl. neighbour, one who dwells near another).

v. 357. *Nemned*, pret. of nemne Mod. E. name, Ag.-S. nemnan, nemnian Germ. nennen, Sw. nämna, »The form nam, with more or less modification, is common to the whole series of Indo Europ. and Finnic languages to the extremity of Siberia »(Wedgwood). The most ancient Germanic form is the Goth. niman.

v. 94. *Pried*, pret. of pry; the origin of it is doubtful; Webster supposes it to be a contraction of per-eye (to eye, to look through); Wedgwood, perhaps more right, from O. Fr. preier, preer, praer (to rob); compare E. *prey* and *prowl*; Chambers thinks it may be a corruption of peer (L. parere).

v. 114. *Prove* Angl.-S. prófian, O. Fr. prover, Fr. prouver, from L. probare; Sw. pröfva, Germ. proben, prüfen.

v. 259. *Passe*, pret. passed v. 154, Fr. passer, It. passare from L. *passus* (a step) pundere, passum (to stretch).

v. 177. *Plese*, M. E. please, O. Fr. plaisir, plesir, Mod. Fr. plaire, It. piacere from L. placere.

v. 244. *Preye*, pret. prayde v. 259; Mod. E. pray, O. Fr. proier, preier, preer, Mod. Fr. prier, It. pregare, from L. precari.

v. 324. *Profer* from L. proferre.

v. 280. *Perceyue*, Mod. E. perceive, Fr. percevoir, fr L. percipere.

v. 370. *Pult*, pret. of pulte with an intrusive *l*. (analogous to *l* in falter, halt, jolt) Mod. E. put, It. bottare, buttare (to cast, to fling), Fr, bouter; probably from Wal. pwtian (to poke to thrust).

v. 339. *Peyned* pp, of peyne, Mod. E. pain Ag.-S. pínan, pínjan (Bosw.), O. N. pína, Sw. pina; the words are probably early introduced from Latin poena, Gr. ποινή; Wedgwood thinks the origin to be the Gr. πόνος labour, in Mod. Gr. bodily pain; Chambers; from the Sanscr. root *pu*, to purify.

v. 205. *Pleide*, pret.; pleyde pp. (v. 350) of pleie, pleye; Mod. E. play, Ag. S. plegan, plegian, (to ply or exercise, to sport); play or plaw signifies boil (according to Wedgwood) *playing* hot, boiling hot. (Ray). Gael. *goil*, boiling, fury. Sp. *bullir*, to boil. Compare also Germ. *pflegen*.

v. 273. *Quake* (to shake); we have placed this verb among the weak verbs, though there is to be found in O. E. a strong preterite quok, Ag. S. cwacian, Du. quacken (to gaggle like a goose), O. N. kvaka (to twitter), Germ. qnackeln (to waver, shake) probably onomatopoet.: compare E. squeak, a. o. Meuller derives it from the same root as O. N. kvika, to move and Germ. quick. (L. vivus).

v. 168. *Quelles*, 3:d pers. sing. pres. af *quelle*. Mod. E. *kill*, Ag. S. cwellan; the form *quell* occurs in Chaucer f. ex.

»And preyid him that he wolde to him sell
Some poison, that he might his rattis *quell*.

Pardoner's Tale.

O. N. kvelja, Sw. qvälja, N. H. G. quälen (cruciare necare); the word is a derivative from the strong Ag. S. cwelan, p. cwæl, pp. cwælen (to be killed); O. H. G. quělan.

v. 314. *Quite*, Fr. quitter, from L. quietus, quiescere.

v. 84. *Rore*, Mod. E. roar, A. S. rárjan; from the sound.

v. 84. *Rente*, preter. of the verb renden. Mod. E. rend, Ag, S. rendan, hrendan, O. N. ræna, to seize by violence.

v. 131. *Reade*. Mod. E. read, Sc. rede (to discourse, to speak at large; — Jamieson); Germ. reden, O. N. roeða, Goth. rêdan, Ag. S. rêdan.

v. 325. *Rekene;* this is one one of the few instances, where the gerund occurs; the gerund is here as in Ag. S. preceded by the particle to (Ag. S. tô); it is, in fact, a

form of the infinitive and probably the dative af it, as it is
evident from the circumstance of its being sometimes used
in passive sense in Ag. S., f. ex. »Is eâc tô witanne þæt
sume gedwolmen wæron, þe woldon» [1] etc. It is besides
to been known, that there are some heretics, who would etc.
The infinit. of this verb must have been reken or reke
from Ag. S. récan, (to regard to care for); akin to Ag. S.
recan, reccan, recnan, Eng. reckon; there is also i O. E.
a form rekken, and recchen, roghte, raughte; the forms
are derived from Goth. *rikan* (Mueller).

v.v. 24, 212. *Seche* (pret. in South E. sogte pp.
isogt), in Ormulum sekenn, M. E. scek, Ag. S. sêcjan,
sêcan, soecan, Sw. sōka, O. N. soekja, Goth. *sokjan*. The
words indicate an old vb. sakan, sok. Concerning the
preterit forms in -ought, O. E. ogte, ohte, we remark that
the final c of the root in Ag. S. was sharpened to h before
the t of the preterit., where the original vowel (to be seen
in the Gothic) reappeared. In present the following »j»
which occasioned a vowel-change, obscured the original
vowel. The g which has been added to the h in the preterite.
may be explained by many analogies. Thus the Ag. S.
wiht is spelled in Eng. wight, Ag. S, cniht, Eng. knight a. s. o.

v. 62. *Sent*, pp. of O. E. senden, M. E. send, Ag. S.
sendan, Goth. sandjan, Sw. sânda. The root seems to be
a lost Goth. verb sinþan (according to Mueller).

v 128. *Studied*, pret. of study, Fr. étudier from the
L. studere (studium).

v. 167. *Schote;* this verb is also spelled *schete* in O.
E. and ought perhaps to have been cited among the strong
verbs, because it had formely a strong flexion; but as only
the infinitive occurs in this romance, it is impossible to
know, whether the preter. and pp. were strong or as in
M. E. weak; M. E. shoot (shot, shot), Ag. S. sceòtan, scò-
tian; Sw. skjuta.

v. 186. *Schewed*, pret. of schewen, Mod. E.; show there
is still a strong pp. in M. E. shown besides the weak
showed, Ag. S. scawjan, sceawjan. Germ. schauen (to look),
Sw. skâda (to behold).

---

[1] See Rask, Grammar of the Anglo-Saxon tongue pp. 105, 106.

v. 193. *Sewède* pret. of sewe, Mod. E. sew (Mueller)
sue, Fr. suivre, It. seguire, from L. *sequi*.

v. 208. *Strecche.* (As to the old forms straught, streight
comp. seche v. 24). Mod. E. stretch, Ag. S. streccan, Sw.
stràcka; Engl. dial. strake, stratch and streak, streek.

v 58. *Seiɡ;* in South E. seggen seyen (Morris); pret.
seide v. 68 seyde v. 343 saide v. 292, sec. pers. seidestow
v. 256; Ag. S. secgan, seggan, Sw. sâga, O. N. segja,
Germ. sagen.

v. 32. *Telle;* 3:d pers. pl. pres. tellen v. 5, tellus v.
187 (tell us) pret. told v. 155; Mod. E. tell, Ag. S. tellan,
O. N. tala, telja, Sw. tala, tälja. An inf. form *tale* occurs v. 158.

v. 239. *Talk,* pr. talked v. 53; dial. talken (to speak
unclearly); comp. Sw. dial. tjola (to speak clumsy as a pea-
sant); Sw. tolka, from the same origin as tell; see above.

v. 315. *Tyde,* pr. tidde v. 187; see bi-tide v. 5.

v. 243. *Turne,* M. E. turn, Ag. S. tyrnan, Fr.
tourner, It. tornare, from Gr. τόρνõς (a pair of compasses)
[Diez].

v. 252. *Tyred,* a shortened form of attyred M. E. atti-
red, pp. of attire; O. Fr. atirer. The Eng. word may be
derived from Ag.-S. tir tyr (splendour).

v. 268. *Tyme* (to befall) Sw. tima; Ag.-S. ge-timian
(to happen).

v. 347. *Tyne* and v. 287 *tine,* to lose; O. N. tyna (to
lose); Ag.-S. teón (loss), tynan, vexare.

v. 288. *Trow* (now only used in present) from Ag.-S.
treówian (to trust), O. N. trûa, Sw. tro, Goth. trauan, Germ.
traucn. The radical meaning is *firm, unyielding* (Wedgwood).

v. 317. *Tauɡt* pret. of teche; concerning the pret. form,
compare, seche v. 24. — Ag.-S. tæcan Germ. zeihen, zeigen;
akin to L. docere Gr. δείχνυμι.

v. 61. *þonkes,* 3:d pers. sing. pres.; þonked v. 101 of
the verb þonken, Mod. E. thank Ag.-S. þancian, þoncian,
Sw. tacka; from the preterit of a Gothic root-verb þigkan
(Mueller).

v. 123. þougt, pret. of þinche, the compound biþougt
v. 279 from bi-þinche. This word is from the same root
as þonke. Comp. Sw. tánka Ag.-S. þencean þyncan.

v. 2. *Woned* (lived), pret. of wonen, also writter wunen
ex. »Genesis and Exodus» v. 469:

> »Jacob on liue *wunede* ðor
> In reste fulle xiiij ger».

Ag.-S. wunian (to dwell), wunung = O. E. woning, Sw.
våning, Germ. wohnung, vb. wohnen. From the past part.
of the old verb wone, wonen the Mod. E. wont (Germ. ge-
wohnt) grew up.

v. 248. *Wende,* v. 218 *wend,* 3:d pers. sing. pres. *wendes*
v. 221; from Ag.-S. *wendan,* to turn; O. N. venda, Germ.
wenden, Goth. vandjan, from the root-verb *vindan* (Mueller).
As to the preterit wente, see *Go.*

v. 17. *Wawe,* M. E. wave from Ag.-S. vagjan; the
change of an old *g* to *w* is not rare, for ex. Ag.-S. dagian,
Eng. dawn a. s. o..

v. 334. *Weped,* v. 35 *wept,* pret. of wepe, Engl. weep
Ag.-S. wepan (to lament, call); this verb was formerly strong
and there is a strong pret. *wep* (v. 48) in this romance.

v. 57. *Wilnen,* 3:d pers. pl. pres. with the peculiar
Midland termination, and wilnes 3:d pers. sing. (v. 254)
of the vb wilnen Ag.-S. *wilnian,* to desire.

v. 70. *Wanted* pret. of wante, Mod. E. want O. N.
vanta; a derivative from the root wan (deficiency, negation)
according to Wedgwood. Compare Ag.-S. *wana,* wanting;
L. *vanus* empty.

v. 74. *Weld;* pret. welt vv. 140, 219 pret. walt (exer-
cised) v. 142; M. E. wield, Ag.-S. gewýldan, geweldan from
the strong Ag.-S. vb *wealdan,* Germ. walten.

v. 92. *Walked,* pp. of walke (or walken) M. E. walk;
already in O. E. this word signifies to go on foot; but the
original meaning is *to roll;* Ag.-S. wealcan, to roll, turn,
tumble; Sw. valka, to roll in the hands.

v. 246. *Worche,* pret. *wrougt* v. 47 and *wrout* v. 112;
Mod. E. work; Ag.-S. wyrcan, wyrcean, pret. worhte; in the
O. E. wrougt and the M. E. wrought the letter *r* has been
transposed (compare: Ag.-S. brid, O. E. bridde M. E. bird).

v. 99. *Warded*, pp. of ward, to keep, O. H. G. wartêu, Sw. vårda; the word went from the Germanic into the Romance languages with the regular change of a Germanic *w* to Rom. *gu*. (Comp. Eng. war, Fr. guerre a. o.); thus the Fr. guarder and It. guardare had great influence upon the M. E. word guard.

v. 113. *Wedded*, pret. of wedden, M. E. wed, from Ag.-S. weddian (to promise, engage); Du. wedden, Germ. wetten (to bet); W. gwedd (a yoke or pair); Goth. vidan (to bind together).

v. 146. *Wayte;* M. E. wait, Sw. vakta, O. H. G. wahtên; from O. N. vaka, to wake (Wedgwood).

v. 264. *Wonde*, to fear, to refrain; from Ag.-S. *wandian*, to fear (Morris) (Sw. våndas?)

v. 293. *White*, to blame; already in Semi-Saxon the transposition of *h* and *w* in the beginning of words was often made; at first the pronunciation did not change, but from such forms as *wo* and *were*, instead of who and where, we may judge that *h* was not generally sounded in a very early period[1]. Ag.-S. witan, witian, to punish, in O. E. witen, (thence probably hwiten, white).

v. 165. *Wited* (took care of) pret. of the vb *wite* to keep, preserve v. 161 wist (in the same sense) from O. E. wisse Ag.-S. wisian (to instruct); wited may be a paralled form of wist.

v. 294. *Werne*, refuse; pret. plur. *werneden* occurs in Genesis and Exodus v. 259; from Ag.-S. wyrnan (to warn) warnian, wærnian; Sw. varna O. H. G. warnôn; from a widely outspread root.

v. 316. *Worþe* (= become), in O. E. the pret. worþed is to be found, and the imp. *»worthe him»* = let him be (Morris). The M. E. gives us but a fragment of this verb; f. ex. in the sense of *betide:*

> Woe *worth* the chase, woe *worth* the day,
> That cost thy life, my gallant grey.
>> Sir Walter Scott, Lady of the Lake.

Ag.-S. weorðan, Germ. werden, Sw. varda = become.

---

[1] Marsh; Lectures on the Engl. language.

v. 89. ɋeme (hide) from Ag.-S. gyman, to take care of, regard; Sw. gömma.

3. *Anomalous verbs.*

v. 72. *Be*, pres. subj.; pres. ind. y *am* (vv. 270, 303), *is* (v. 231), nis (= ne is) v. 366, plur. ɋe *arn* (v. 104), *bestow*, pres. subj. (v. 333); pret. was (v. 278), nas (= ne was) (vv. 81, 216), subj. *where* (v. 250), instead of were (comp. white v. 293), past p. be (»nad he be» v. 152) with rejected *n*. This verb is considered as anamalous, but it might perhaps more properly have been called defect at least in its Mod. E. form. It is derived from two different roots namely from the Ag.-S. verbs beón (to be to become) and wesan (to be); the verb beón had formerly a future sense; and *be* had only the power of a present form, where the form *am* was not to be found [2]). In the Slavonie languages the same roots are found with the same power. The third pers. sing. indicative present and past of the substantive verb (is and was) terminate in *s*, because the were used so already in Angl.-Saxon. The Normans could not pronounce *th*, which is the old ending of the verbs, but gave it the *s* or rather *z* sound, which is most often the present sound of this letter in the third pers. sing. Thus Mr. Marsh thinks that this circumstance and the old ending in *s* of the most important verb *to be*, occasioned its general adoption in that inflexion. — The present ind. plural has in this romance the form *arn*, this form occurs for the first time in English in the Ormulum on pp. 157 and 237 of the first volume, where it is spelled *aren*. It is from Scandinavian origin. Even Chaucer only twice employs this form. The old Ag.-S. plur. forms were beôð (of beôn) and synd, syndon (of wesen).

v. 286. *Con* and v. 233 *kan*, pres.; pret. *couɋþe* v. 116, *couɋde* v. 118, *couþe* v. 17, of the O. E. verb cunnen (to know, to be able); in M. E. the infinitive is not used; the word is derived from L. gnoscere, noscere, Gr. γνῶναι (E. Mueller). The most remarkable with this verb is the

---

[2] Latham, the English language p. 552.

preterite; the ꞡ in couꞡþe is probably a dialectical propriety, as I have not found it elsewhere in O. E., but if we regard the pret. *couþe*, Ag.-S. *cuðe*, we will at once find, that there is no reason for the *l* in the M. E. could; this *l* was a blunder of spelling and was introduced to match the *l* in *should* and *would*.

v. 129. *Do*, pret. *dede* v. 338, gerund to done, with the peculiar ending, v. 309, Ag.-S. dôn Gr. τίθημι; the second *d* in dede is probably a remain of the reduplication.

v. 294. *Dorst;* in sense dorst, M. E. durst, is both a present and a preterite, as we can say: I durst not, in the sense, I am afraid to, and I was afraid to (according to Latham); but it is most often employed as a preterite; the present is *dare* in M. E.; the root of this verb is found in Gr. θαρρεῖν; the *s* in dorst is most probably part of the original word. The word occurs in most Teutonic languages.

v. 65. *Go*, *goþ* v. 260, 3:d pers. sing. pres. (with the old ending); imper. goþ vv. 252, 255, preter. *wente* v. 87, went v. 63, pp. wente v. 365; the pret. wente, M. E. went and the pp. wente, used in this romance, are borrowed from the verb wende, see v. 248 *wende*. In South. E. there is a preterite eode. Goth. gaggan O. N. ganga, Germ. gehen Sw. gå.

v. 312. *May*, pret. *miꞡt* (vv. 14, 83 a. o.); O. N. mega Sw. må, Goth. magan; the same root in Gr. μέγας, L. magnus; Ag.-S. mágan, pret. mihte, meahte, from which the O. E. mit, Mod. E. might has come.

v. 120. *Ouꞡt*, Mod. E. ought, origin. a preterite, also used as a present, Ag.-S. âhte from the Ag.-S. verb âgan, E. owe.

v. 242. *Schal, schalstow* v. 314, schaltow v. 329. pret. schold v. 99, schuld v. 212; schal is originally a strong preterite, as well as *can*, may, ought and wite. In Mod E. there are seven such preterit-presents, namely: can, dare, may, must, ought, shall, weet, the latter rather obsolete. Ag.-S. sculan, pret. scolde, sceolde, from which it is apparent, that the *l* belongs to the root.

vv. 76, 157. *Wol* pres., (Mod. E. will, plur. wol v. 128 (with rejected *n*); pret. wolde v. 43, wold v. 56, plur. wolden

v. 152, Mod. E. would; from Ag.-S. willan, pret. wolde; there are in the other Indo-Europ. languages forms spelled with *e* and other forms spelled with *i*; Goth. viljan, Germ. wollen, O. N. vilja, L. volo, velle, Russ. volja (will, wish, concent, Gr. βούλεσθαι.

v. 246. *Wite* (to know), wite pres. subj., vv. 35, 270, witow pres. subj. v. 66, wot * 1:st pers. pres. ind. v.v. 103, 291 not (ne wot) v. 309, pret. wiste v. 143; from Ag.-S. witan, pres. wât, pret. wiste and wisse; Mod. E. weet, Sw. veta, pret. visste; Germ. wissen; akin to L. videre (to see).

The authors chiefly referred to in the preparation of this dissertation are:

Bosworth; A compendious Anglo-Saxon and English Dictionary London 1848.

Chambers's Etymological Dictionary of the English Language, edited by J. Donald. Edinb. 1869.

Craik; History of English Literature and of English Language. London 1861.

Latham; The English Language.

Lidforss; A Survey of the English Conjugation. Upsala 1863.

Marsh; Origin and History of the English Language and of the Early Literature it embodies. London 1862.

Marsh; Lectures on the English Language. London 1863.

Morris; Specimens of Early English. Oxford 1867.

Max Müller; Vorlesungen über die Wissenschaft der Sprache, bearbeitet v. Böttger. Leipzig 1866.

Mueller E.; Etymologisches Wörterbuch der Englischen Sprache. Cöthen 1865, 67.

Rask; Grammar of the Anglo-Saxon Tongue; translated by Thorpe. London 1865.

Schwenck; Wörterbuch der Deutschen Sprache in Beziehung auf Ableitung und Begriffsbildung. Frankf. 1855.

Wedgwood; Dictionary of English Etymology. London 1859, 62, 65.

---

* Originally a strong preterite.